TENDER WORLDS

TALES OF THE REAL AND SURREAL

Evan Bruce • Koker Christensen
D. Joel Dick • Edan Howell

YORKLAND PUBLISHING

YP

Published by
Yorkland Publishing
12 Tepee Court
Toronto, Ontario M2J 3A9
Canada

www.yorklandpublishing.com

ISBN: 978-1-7390044-3-9

Edited by Ed Shiller

Cover and Text Design by Rosemary Shiller

Printed and bound by IngramSpark

CONTENTS

PREFACE

Our small group – a short story club – was formed from a desire to get together over drinks and discuss literature. Knowing that life would likely get in the way, trying to read novels seemed a recipe for failure. We just knew that the text wouldn't get read.

Edan Howell had the solution: short stories. Over the next decade, we tried to meet once a month and probably met about eight times a year.

Starting with Chekhov, we initially followed a syllabus of the acknowledged greats in the genre. We developed a deeper appreciation of the dark storytelling of Flannery O'Connor and the fantastic pacing of Edgar Allen Poe. Once we completed the syllabus, we chose stories to read on a rotating basis.

Over the years, our discussions evolved beyond the stories themselves. We delved into the historical context, the personal lives of the authors, and the various interpretations and critiques of the texts. These meetings became a sanctuary for intellectual exchange, where each story was a portal to broader conversations about human nature, society, and the art of storytelling itself.

Our gatherings were more than just book club meetings; they were evenings filled with laughter, heated debates, and moments of shared insight. The camaraderie we built over these sessions was as enriching as the stories we read. It was in this intimate setting that our creative impulses were nurtured, leading us to pen our own tales.

This anthology is a testament to our journey – a decade of literary exploration, friendship, and creative experimentation. We hope our stories, much like those we have cherished, will ignite the imagination and provoke thoughtful reflection in our readers.

D. Joel Dick

ALL IN A DAY'S WORK

By Evan Bruce

I was born out of a flash of fire and immediately started heading towards Earth. As fast as possible. It took eight minutes and twenty seconds.

The planet's defence system, if you could call it that, consists of a wispy layer of cloud. I blow past this like it's not even there.

On I go to Switzerland, straight towards an office with a big bay window. This office has a door, but I'm a path-of-least-action type of guy, so I go straight through the window. I don't even tap the brakes; full speed, I hit this thing. Again, it may as well not have been there. It didn't slow me down one bit.

I whiz past this clerk with a wack-a-doodle haircut. He doesn't even blink. Then I smash my face directly into a clock. I cannot tell you what material that clock face is made of, but I can say that it is unforgiving. I bounce off that thing so hard that I'm sent careening backwards as fast as I went in.

Now, you're gonna think I'm making this next part up, but I'm not. I stared at that clock for a long time. Forever, actually. And for the entire time, that second hand did not move.

BOYS WILL BE BAD

(And the Rest May Be Even Worse)

By Evan Bruce

It was Mark who had noticed certain teachers were lazy about locking the windows on the top row. Some of them were old or fat, or both, so standing on a waist-high ledge to reach the locks wasn't in the cards for them. When he told Sean and me about this observation on our walk home from school, we both instantly knew what he was thinking.

We recruited Rich into our B & E squad since we knew he was down for this type of fun and could be trusted to keep his mouth shut. Some of our friends were cool guys that we liked hanging out with, but they had this ridiculous habit of telling their parents shit they shouldn't, for no good goddamn reason at all. Like, why would you tell your mom we're going to egg Dale Markewitz's house, Derek, you blabbermouth idiot? No way was he going to be invited to join the team.

We all met up at Rich's house to plan our first mission since, after getting divorced, his mom was barely ever home. Also, he had this cool makeshift shooting range in his backyard for his BB guns, and an oscar in his room, which is kinda like a piranha that you could feed small fish to, always a kick to watch.

We agreed dark clothing was a good idea since this was going to be done under the cover of night, of course. Our cover story was that we were headed to Jack Darling Park to chuck around this glow-in-the-dark frisbee that Sean had, but we could have made up any bullshit story. I mean, how are our parents going to keep track of what four fifteen-year-olds on bikes are doing in the suburbs? They can't. Our stories just had to match.

We also agreed that we had to get inside, leave no trace, and get out quickly. If we spray-painted a bunch of shit on the chalkboard or smashed computers, there would be a tonne of heat from the police, and none of us wanted that.

Our first target was our old elementary school, Tecumseh. It was close, and we all knew it like the back of our hand. Plus, fuck that place! So, on a Friday night, we all put on dark-coloured hoodies and dark pants and then met up at Rich's house. Our mood was electric. We felt like we were onto something great. The other kids would be doing what that night? Getting drunk at the fire pit by the broken bridge in the forest, like we needed to see Heather McKonkee puke her guts out yet again. We were onto something that would test us, and like Billy the Kid says in Young Guns: "You have to test yourself every day, gentlemen. Once you stop testing yourself, you get slow. And when that happens … they kill you."

We decided the best place to attempt entry was the south side of the school. There were these ten-foot-tall cedar hedges blocking anyone's view. Right away, Sean spotted a window that was open a few inches. It was high up, sure, but fifteen-year-olds in good shape are like ninjas, so it was a cinch for us. The only one who had trouble was Mark, who was the tallest and in the best shape from all the rep hockey he played. The problem was his size. We referred to him as the "Ukrainian Ox." Squeezing through the window was a challenge, but he finally made it.

Once inside the classroom, we all felt a rush. There was light from the street lamps so that after our eyes adjusted, we could navigate the classroom pretty well without flashlights, which we all agreed would draw too much attention – though I did bang my balls against a desk corner, which the other guys thought was hilarious. We stuck to the plan and didn't mess with or steal anything, though Mark found a bunch of microscopes, and I knew he was tempted to take one because he loved checking out bugs close up. There was a short discussion about going into other classrooms since we were already in the school, but Rich figured they had hidden motion sensors in the hallways. I suspected that was bullshit, but I wasn't willing to test my theory. So we got the fuck out of there the same way we got in and went to the nearby Becker's to get some drinks and candy. Rich also grabbed the latest copy of *Guns & Ammo*. There was some cool shit in that magazine.

What followed was an unprecedented run of B&Es in Mississauga, and I doubt it will ever be equalled. Do you have any idea how many schools there are in this town? A shitload. And we got into every single one of them. Never people's homes, never any businesses, only schools. Because they were empty and…fuck them.

We had to learn to deal with schools that had no open windows. This one school, Port Credit, our high school's rival, never had one open window, even when it was so hot that your balls were covered in sweat all day. I had the brilliant idea to bring along a glass-cutting tool my mom used for her stained-glass window projects. Turns out these school windows are not made of regular glass but some type of plexiglass, which the cutter just scratched. It was Mark who figured out that a small crowbar, small enough to fit into a backpack, would easily overmatch the cheap locks secured by two tiny screws. That innovation made us unstoppable. Take that, Port Credit, you security-conscious motherfuckers.

Then, one night, while we were all in Rich's room waiting for his oscar to eat this goldfish, Mark tells the group he wants to head back to Tecumseh to grab one of these microscopes. They had twenty of the fucking things, so would they notice if one went missing? We figured they wouldn't. As long as he covered up the "Property of Tecumseh P.S." written on the side, he could just tell his parents he bought it at a garage sale. No sweat. Sean protested a little bit, but Mark and I convinced the group this wouldn't be a problem. I was on Mark's side because I also wanted to take something, a ream of paper. See, I was big into writing and drawing my comic books, and I was working on this new one about this gang of super-hot ninjas with big tits that could be hired to take out assholes, like the A-Team in feudal Japan. A project like that required a lot of paper, and the cost was adding up.

I worked at McDonald's making the Big Macs and shit, but

I had other expenses like BMX bike parts, going to the movies, you know, shit like that. And, once again, these classrooms usually had a cupboard with stacks of these reams, so no one would notice one gone. So off we went. The mission was a complete success, and if you haven't seen a praying mantis' head up close, you really should; it's fucking amazing.

One thing you should know about me is that my fucktard parents make me go to church every Sunday. I fucking hate it. I refuse to call it "Going to Church" and instead refer to it as "Going to the Cult meeting." And we don't just go to the cult meetings; we are deep into it. My dad is an Elder in this bullshit cult, and my mom sings in the choir. And guess who has to stand there every Sunday morning and greet the wrinkled old hags who dip themselves in perfume? I mean, are they hoping our Lord and Savior can smell them up in heaven?

So, take a wild guess about how thrilled I was when my dipshit English teacher tells us we all have to read Fifth Business by Robertson Davies. Do you know what it's about? Saints. I shit you not. I fucking hated it. So, one day I'm at my locker, super grumpy that I had to read this crappy book, and my buddy Chad asked me why I was in such a bad mood. I tell him about having to read this piece of shit novel, and in response, he hands me the Autobiography of Malcolm X. That book fucking rocks.

Chad's a white dude, but he loves playing basketball and, as a result, hangs out with the handful of black kids who go to our school, and they're feeding him all sorts of great recommendations when it comes to music and books and shit. They turn him onto Public Enemy, which quickly becomes his favourite band. I mean, I don't know if you can call them a band since none of them plays an instrument, but the music is awesome and a welcome change for a bunch of us who are sick and tired of all of the Tragically Hip and Steve Miller that plays at every fucking party.

So, to show my gratitude for the book recommendation, I concocted this plan to make Chad a thank-you gift – a necklace. You see, Public Enemy is, as far as I can tell, run by this guy Chuck D. He's the serious political guy. But I guess to add a bit of levity, there's this other rapper there called Flavor Flav. It's hard to describe this dude because he's fucking weird, but all you need to know is that he always wears a necklace with a big-ass clock on it. I don't know why. Maybe there's some reason, something to do with slavery? Who the fuck knows? Doesn't matter.

The point is, I'm going to make Chad one of these necklaces…the best one ever. The chain part is easy. My dad makes me go to the hardware store with him all the time. He figures knowing how to use tools and fix shit is part of being a man, some shit like that. So, I know I can go to the back left corner of the store where they got all sorts of chains on spools. You buy it by the foot. But what about the clock? I want a big one. And do you know where you can find huge clocks? High up on the wall, in every single classroom in every single school in the whole goddamn country. So, it's back to Tecumseh we go.

At this point, our crew had their shit screwed on so tight that I knew this would be a breeze. I told the guys my plan, and they were all on board. We met up at Rich's house on a Friday night, more psyched than usual because we were all goal-driven people and liked to have a purpose. But something seriously fucked up happened before we could leave Rich's place. His mom, who had recently remarried, ordered Rich to include his new stepbrother in our night Frisbee game. We all hated this idea. You see, we knew this kid from school. His name was Jimmy Graham, and he was a slimy little weasel. I, in particular, protested vigorously because I had a history with this fucking asshole.

Last semester, our French class went on a ski trip to Quebec. On one of the nights, they put on a dance at the hotel. Seriously? A dance? What are we, in grade eight? Fuck off with that shit. I wanted to sneak out to find one of these head shops that will sell you porno mags and butterfly knives, but attendance at this retarded event was mandatory. So, I sat on a chair in the corner and talked to my buddy Derek about the day's skiing. Yeah, he's a blabbermouth, but his mom wasn't around, and he's a shit-hot good skier. I figured they could make me attend the dance, but they couldn't make me dance. And then this girl, Katie Skillen, walked up and asked me to dance. Katie had blonde hair, a really pretty face, a figure skater's bum, and she was wearing this tight, black turtleneck sweater. It looked like her tits were trying to bust out of that sweater and might eventually do it. So, I said, "Yes."

When we started to dance, she pulled me in close, like, fully ramming her tits into my chest. I had never had this happen before while dancing with a girl, but for some reason, I got a rock-hard boner. You can't control those things. I tried to put a little distance between us because I was embarrassed, but she just pulled me right back in. There was no escape. Afterwards, I thanked her for the dance and made a beeline straight back to Derek to tell him what happened. I mean, I was mortified this had happened, but if you think about it, it was her fault for pushing those perfect tits into me. But, to my great relief, Derek (who has way more experience with girls than me) explained that they love that. It shows them they're hot and you're into them. Alright, these girls are a black box-like mystery to me, but Derek seemed to know what he was talking about, so I stopped worrying about it.

On the bus ride back from the ski resort, I just wanted to sleep. On the last night, me and a couple of the other guys did sneak out and find a head shop. They sold us porno mags, butterfly knives, and a bunch of beer, so I was hungover. I figured I'd sleep at the back of the bus where there were three seats together, which would make a decent bed of sorts. Before I could fall asleep, Katie asked me if she could sit with me. I told her I planned to sleep so I wouldn't be good company, but she offered to let me rest my head on her lap, so I said, "Sure." It was pretty nice. She ran her fingers through my hair, which helped me doze off. I wasn't awake for it, but Derek told me one goofball tried to write on my face with a Sharpie, but Katie wouldn't allow it, which I thought was pretty cool.

The following Monday, at school, Katie asked me to take her on a date, which I did. We went for burgers at the Satellite Diner and then went to see the movie Dead Again. Great flick, check it out if you haven't seen it. While driving her home, I had to explain the movie. There's a bit of a twist at the end, and it started to dawn on me that Katie wasn't too bright. When we got to her place, she invited me in. Turns out her parents were out that night, and I knew what she wanted to do. The idea terrified me. What if she gets pregnant? Or I get AIDS? Or, worst of all, I suck shit at this sex thing, and she tells all her friends? Fuck that action. I gave some lame excuse and got the hell out of there.

We never dated again. One of her cheerleading buddies asked me the next day if I was a fag, and I mumbled something about Katie being dumber than a fence post, and that was the end of it. I found out later she had been Jimmy's girlfriend during the ski trip, but had dumped him over the phone when she got home.

Jimmy was pissed at me for causing the breakup, which is bullshit since she was the one who asked me to dance and created the whole boner incident. But that little weasel was too stupid to understand the distinction.

So, the idea of bringing this shifty twerp with us on our mission strikes me as being all kinds of bad news, but what the fuck could we do? Rich's mom was a nice lady, and here she is, trying to make this second marriage work. Plus, we couldn't think of any good reason not to bring Jimmy along for a Frisbee game, nor could we explain what we were really up to, so we all went along with it.

How many times on the walk to Tecumseh did I explain to that little shit how important it was that he NEVER tell anyone what we did that night? Six. Maybe seven. Enough times, the message would've been received loud and clear by someone with a functioning brain.

When we got to the school, we went straight to the area shielded by the cedars, found an open window, and all of us scrambled up and through the window. Once inside, we quickly determined that the clock was so high that only Mark would be able to reach it, and then only when we moved the teacher's desk underneath it. Mark's handy crowbar made prying it off the wall dick easy, but we hit a snag. You see, those clocks are not battery-powered, they're wired into the school's electrical system. One wire in, one wire out. No problem, I figure. I look in the teacher's desk drawer and find a pair of big metal scissors.

Turns out Mark's dad wasn't as big a believer in teaching his son how mechanical shit works as my dad was, so guess what the lug-head Ukrainian Ox does? Instead of cutting one wire at a time, like I figured he would do, he cuts both simultaneously. Boom. Big flash. Mark goes flying back and crashes into a bunch of desks. Oh, man – the smell. We all go into panic mode. Mark is on the ground, somehow holding the clock in one hand and the scissors in the other. He's not moving. Fuck. This is so bad.

This image flashes in my mind of me explaining to Mark's parents that he died while trying to help me make a Flavor Flav necklace. And they're none too happy about it. Thank fucking Christ, Mark comes to, and aside from some minor burns on his scissor hand, he's okay. So, I chuck the clock into my backpack, and we get the fuck out of there.

Ah, fuck. I almost forgot to tell you about an important part of the story. One of the guys in our group had this, uh, special talent. He could shit on command. I can't tell you which one of us it is because we all swore an oath never to reveal this person's identity. Anyway, he was always on the lookout for situations to put this talent to use. One time, and I think this is the funniest example, we were walking home late one night from a party and discovered a car parked in a driveway that wasn't locked. We searched the car for cash or other valuable stuff, but didn't find much. Before continuing our walk home, this guy decides it would be funny to take a shit on the driver's seat. So, he did. Imagine being the owner of that car and coming out the next morning to go to work. Oh, man, we laughed about that for a long time. So, after grabbing the clock, but before leaving the classroom, this guy took a shit in the teacher's desk drawer. Imagine the look on that teacher's face when they discovered that on Monday morning. Fucking priceless.

Necklace construction was easy, and I think it turned out pretty well. I'm sorry to report that when I gave Chad the necklace on Monday morning, he was less than impressed. First, it was stupidly heavy, in his opinion. Second, everybody knew those types of clocks were from a school and, therefore, obviously stolen property. He stashed it in his locker and threw me a quick "Thanks a lot" in a tone that didn't indicate the kind of gratitude I'd been hoping for.

Meanwhile, what is Jimmy I-Have-Dog-Shit-For-Brains Graham doing that morning? He is bragging to some do-gooder bitches in his class about how he got to hang out with me, Sean, and Rich on Friday night AND that we broke into Tecumseh to steal a clock. I have no clue why he left Mark out of the story, and I don't care. I just hope Jimmy marries a girl that looks like Katie before having kids, and that after having kids, she ends up looking like Danny DeVito's portrayal of the Penguin. Because fuck that guy, big time. One of these idiot chicks went and told her parents the story Jimmy told them, and then, for whatever fucked-up reason, the dad called the police and passed on the information.

Now, what would one of these shithead Peel Regional Police officers normally do after getting a phone call from a parent passing along a second-hand rumour from a high school student about a low-level crime like clock theft? Thank the citizen for calling, promise to bring the perpetrators to justice, and then hang up the phone and immediately forget about it. But, no, this was a seriously fucked-up time in Mississauga.

You see, a couple of weeks before that phone call to the cops, someone had burned down the Sikh temple on Indian Road. All the cops had to go on was one witness who lived nearby who had seen "a small group of teenage boys" fleeing the scene in the dead of night. Everybody thought it was a hate crime. No way was Mayor Hazel McCallion going to let this type of crap go down in her town. For sure, she dragged the Chief of Police into her office and told him to shake the trees until the guilty parties were brought to justice. This was priority level number one, and the Chief Idiot's job was on the line.

So now these Keystone cop motherfuckers are off their leashes, but their only lead is that teenage boys are responsible. They don't have a description of any of the boys, nor even a solid number of how many are involved. Good luck with your investigation, Officer Dicklick.

Two days after that fucking phone call, I was sitting there in French class, admiring the teacher's ass. Mme. Tyssen was one of my favourite teachers. She had grown up in Quebec and had graduated from teacher's college only two years prior, so she was the youngest teacher at our school. And she was a stone-cold fox. On that particular day, she was wearing these navy-blue pants that hugged her gravity-defying ass like Saran Wrap. She was writing something on the blackboard about verb conjugation, but I was focused solely on the fact that, yet again, there was no visible panty line. How could that be in those pants? In my mind, there were only two ways for that to be possible. Either she was wearing an impossibly tiny thong, or she was going commando. And, yes, I had a boner. Again, her fault, not mine.

You know how those classroom doors have a small window with some sort of wire mesh between the panes? Someone tapped on that little window, and when we all looked to see who it was, we saw Sean's worried face. He looked straight at me and motioned for me to come out to the hallway.

"Uh, est-ce que je peux aller aux toilettes?" I asked. Mme. Tyssen knew Sean and I were friends and gave me a flat, "Non." So I looked back to Sean, shook my head, and raised my hands a bit, palms upturned, to indicate, "Sorry, bro. Not gonna happen." Sitting next to me, one row over, was Roger Gallant. We were friends, but like, C-level friends. He never phoned me, and I never phoned him, but we would hang out at parties and shoot the shit. He asked if he could "aller aux toilettes," and Mme. Foxy said, "Oui."

He came back four minutes later, sat down at his desk, turned to me, and whispered, "The cops arrested Sean, and he says they're coming for you next." That hit me like a bucket of ice-cold water and gave me a terrible feeling in the pit of my stomach. The remaining twenty minutes of that class seemed to pass at an agonizingly slow pace. I can't even begin to tell you what type of terrible thoughts were creeping into my brain. Just…horrible shit.

The next class was gym, which Sean and I had together. For a while, this sweet, meek teacher in training had been observing the class, and that day was going to be the first class she took over and taught on her own. Her brilliant idea was to have us play flag football outside on the actual football field. At no point during that class did she have command and control. The rest of the guys played a game of tackle football without any regard for the score while Sean and I stood on the fifty-yard line as he proceeded to lay out just what the fuck had happened.

That morning, Sean had been sitting in science class, hoping that Mr. Creepy wasn't going to give him yet another impromptu, unrequested shoulder rub, when two cops showed up at the door. They explain to the teacher that they're there to arrest Sean. They slap the cuffs on him and march him to the principal's office. Sean was light on the details of what went on in the office, but apparently, it was a short meeting, and then he was transported by cruiser to the Division 11 cop shop. Once he got there, Sean was put into an interrogation room and told to remove his belt and shoelaces. They didn't want him to kill himself, they explained. Then they left him there for fifteen minutes by himself in an otherwise empty room except for a table, a few chairs, and a big clock on the wall. If you thought all sorts of bad shit was going through my head during French class, imagine what was going through Sean's head then. Nothing good.

Eventually, two different cops come into the room, detectives this time. They tell Sean that before arresting him, they had arrested me. They said they put me in the same interrogation room and explained to me that an anonymous tip had helped them figure out that we had broken into Tecumseh and stolen the clock, at which point I confessed to the whole thing. Since I had confessed, if Sean didn't confess, they would tell the judge he hadn't cooperated and as a result, the judge would come down on him like a tonne of bricks.

Now, note that at no point while the police are interrogating Sean, who is a minor, was there a parent, legal guardian, or lawyer present. That's illegal. And a clear violation of Sean's rights as a citizen of Canada. Also, note that at no point during the rest of this story do any of our parents bring this up. Nor do our lawyers.

At that point, Sean, who I guess has never seen an episode of Law & Order in his life and therefore had no idea this is exactly the type of unethical crap these asshole cops pull, confesses. The cops videotaped the whole thing. I can't blame him. I'm glad they arrested him first because I might've done the same.

Now it gets really interesting. Detective Dickhead number one tells Sean that they will drop all charges and make this all go away if he tells them who burned down the temple. Both cops start working him hard, going on about how they know kids brag about this stuff, and surely Sean heard something, and don't worry, buddy, we'll make sure your name never comes up in court, and so on. The problem was that Sean had no idea who burned it down, so no deal. Dickhead number one left in a huff, and Dickhead number two changed his demeanour to Mr. Nice Guy. He pushes a big pile of file folders in front of Sean and tells him that he's a good boy for confessing and the cops are going to tell the judge he cooperated, sort of. If Sean wants a glowing report of cooperation from them, he has to go through every open B&E investigation involving a school and tell them which ones we were responsible for. He assures Sean we won't be charged with any of these crimes; they just want to close the files and put the manpower to use on other crimes. So, Sean, believing this asshole, doesn't ever open or read any of the files. He just tells the cop they were all of us. All sixty-five of them.

After that, they finally contacted Sean's parents to come pick him up. While waiting for them to arrive Dickhead number two revealed to Sean the lie about arresting me. Sean is to stay at home and not have any contact with me. After what was, I'm sure, a super fun car ride home, Sean made up some bullshit excuse about having a test at school and then came straight to my French class.

My fucking head was reeling from this goddamn information dump Sean was laying on me. Somewhere near the middle of his story, the teacher in training came up to us and instructed us to join the football game, but before we could respond, one of the other guys threw a perfect spiral that hit her smack in the back of her head, so she fucked off to find the culprit. She never did.

The walk home from school that day was like a death march. I knew I had to tell my parents what had happened, and every step brought me closer to that nightmare of a task. The conversation went about as well as I figured it would. They weren't as angry as you might think. Their reaction was a brutal combination of stunned disbelief and profound disappointment. I kinda wish they had gotten mad instead. We called the cops and told them I would turn myself in the next morning. And these cops, being the nice guys they are, sent a cruiser to our house the next morning to pick me up. My parents loved having the neighbours see that.

My experience at Division 11 was more streamlined than Sean's. They put me in the interrogation room and immediately launched into the same bullshit about dropping all charges if I'd tell them who burned down the temple. No joy, dickheads. I didn't have a clue, and thank God, because no one wants to be a rat. I can't tell you what happened to Rich because after his arrest, his mom transferred him to a military academy and we never saw or heard from him again. He did love guns, so hopefully, that went alright for him. Fuck, his poor mom. What a shit life she had.

If you've never been to court, you might not know that you don't immediately go to trial. First, you have to enter a plea. Both of our parents made the brilliant decision not to hire us lawyers and told us to enter guilty pleas. Sean got called first and entered his guilty plea, and after a few other kids entered theirs (all "not guilty"), I did the same. No trial for guilty pleas, straight to sentencing, which is done in another room at the courthouse. While we were waiting for our turns, we got to see a bunch of other kids get sentenced, and honestly, watching that made me feel a whole lot better. These other kids were all hardcore delinquents. We easily had committed the least egregious crime on the docket that day. One guy had been seriously fucked up on a bunch of drugs and tried to stab his mom with a steak knife. And that wasn't his first crime by a long shot. He got six months' probation and had to get counselling of some sort. We were first-time, non-violent offenders. I mean, seriously, the window had been open, so it wasn't even breaking, just entering and grand theft clock. And, not only had we confessed, but we also had Dickheads number one and two vouching for us. The judge was this sweet old lady with a calm, sympathetic demeanour. She reminded me so much of a grandma that I even looked to see if she had a glass bowl of hard candy up on the bench.

Then Sean got called up. The crown prosecutor went through the crime we had confessed to in great detail, and then tagged on that we had also admitted to sixty-five other counts of B&E. Fucking great. Thanks a lot, you lying dickhead cops. Oh, the crown also throws in a mention of the shit in the desk drawer. What the fuck? Is that even a crime?

Sweet, old grandma suddenly transformed into a

stern-as-hell rage machine. She went off on Sean like he had been running an international child porn ring. She started going on about how Sean had this great family life, and there was no reason on Earth for him to be wasting this court's precious time. She even did something she didn't do to any other kid there that day. She made him turn around and look at his mother, sobbing in the gallery. Then she sentenced him to one year of probation, and fifty hours of community service, and slapped on a non-association clause with me. If you've never heard of that punishment before, don't feel bad. Neither had I. It meant that Sean and I couldn't be within 100 metres of each other, except at school, and even then, we were not to speak to each other or have any other form of contact. You know, in case we got together and hatched a plan to steal a stapler.

It was the worst punishment handed out that day to the kid who had committed the least serious crime. Wonderful judgment on the part of that wrinkled old hag wearing the robe, wouldn't you agree? Seeing Sean get fucked over like that shook my parents so badly that they decided we should hire a lawyer. After I had already entered a guilty plea. Way to go, mom and dad.

When I got called up, the public defender explained our change in plans and asked for a continuance, which we got. We hired a criminal defence attorney, and not only was she this young, cute, blonde woman, but she had what I thought was a really good plan: Let's do the judge's job for her. Have my parents impose probationary-like measures on me, immediately start doing volunteer community service, and go to Tecumseh and apologize to the principal and pay for a replacement clock. When we present this all to the judge, she'll (hopefully) give me a suspended sentence.

My parents did the first part and grounded me for a year. I had to do the other two parts myself. The meeting with the principal was the worst part. First of all, if you can believe it, one of those clocks costs $382. What the fuck is that clock made out of? Titanium and diamonds? Second, he wanted to know what we had against the teacher. It must be something, otherwise, why take a shit in her desk drawer? I tried to explain that we didn't even know that woman, she started after we had left that place. He didn't buy it, and it's safe to say he did not accept my apology. Okay, that meeting sucked big time, but it was all done now, so bring on the suspended sentence.

The big day arrived, and I was feeling pretty good about my chances. I was in my 'I'm a responsible citizen' suit and tie, we had all of the supporting documentation about community service and restitution ready to go, and my lawyer even had on these gray slacks that fit the same way as Mme. Tyssen's blue pants. I thought this suspended sentence was in the bag. Then I got called up before the judge, the same one as before. My lawyer laid out all of the stuff I had done to atone, and then I received my sentence. That old battleaxe, who probably hasn't been properly fucked in thirty years, says she remembers me and Sean and launches into this fucking speech about how she couldn't care less about all this crap I've done over the last six months to atone. I did the same crime as Sean, so I'm getting the same fucking punishment. Thanks a lot for the legal advice, blondie and by the way, your panty line is totally visible. There are no words to express how furious I was at this outcome.

Probation wasn't that bad. I was lucky that my probation officer was a young woman who treated me pretty well. I got the indication she looked forward to our meetings. How is school going? Good, I'm on the honour roll, again, on track to be an Ontario Scholar. And how is life at home? Great. My dad, my brother, and I are going fishing next weekend. She quickly switched our meetings from weekly to monthly. Community service sucks, but you just put your head down and grind it out. After thirty hours, my probation officer decided I'd done enough.

The non-association clause was the worst part. I feel compelled to mention, just to show what a fucked up legal system we have in Canada, that when Sean was sleeping in his bed, and I was sleeping in mine, we were in violation of the clause. He lived across the street from me, you dumb fuck judge.

I can't end the story without telling you about one last thing. Last week I was at a party at Roger's house. My probation had ended almost a year ago, so nobody brought up my legal troubles anymore. Even I had stopped thinking about it very much. Because of the Young Offenders Act, my criminal record would be expunged five years after my sentence ended. That meant by the time I graduated from university and started applying for real jobs, I'd have a clean record, so all worries about ruining my life had faded away.

So, when Sean came up and asked me if I wanted to smoke a joint with him and Paul Cunningham, who was a funny guy and easily the smartest guy from the Druggie Burnout crew, I said, "Sure." Behind Roger's house is a small forest, and Sean insisted we go there to burn this dube. I thought it was overkill, but whatever, a small break from the Tragically Hip blaring at full volume suited me just fine. Sean sparked up the joint, took a couple of hauls, then passed it to Paul and said, "Tell my buddy here what you just told me."

Paul proceeds to tell me about the time he and three of his friends broke into the Sikh temple on Indian Road a couple of years ago. Well, they didn't break in. They discovered the back door was unlocked, so they went in and dropped acid. They got so fucked up that they put on some robes they found and started to fuck around with the candles.

One of his friends tripped and knocked the table full of lit candles into a floor-to-ceiling curtain. The way he tells it, the whole place was engulfed in flames five minutes later since none of them had the wherewithal to grab a fire extinguisher, and probably couldn't have operated the goddamn thing properly even if they had, given how fucked up they were. So, they hightailed it out of there, booked it straight to Paul's house, and made a pact never to tell anyone about it.

And they got away with it, because no one from their crew went to school on Monday morning or bragged about it to some tattletale chick with a goddamn Good Samaritan for a dad.

CHESTERMAN BEACH

By Koker Christensen

The boy's grandma lived in Tofino, in a cabin on Chesterman Beach. By 1978, she'd had enough of things in Vancouver, so she picked up and moved to the edge of Canada. If you're travelling west, it's the last stop before Japan.

He spent a month there one summer. His dad drove him up in the Volvo. On the ferry crossing from Horseshoe Bay to Nanaimo, they ate hamburgers served under domed metal plate covers, which seemed very fancy to the boy. And his dad gave him quarters for video games. When they got off, they drove the winding road to Tofino, stopping once when the boy felt carsick.

His grandma's place was green and thick and damp. A narrow path through the bushes led from the road to the cabin. The porch was full of treasures retrieved from the shore. Glass balls – floats from Japanese fishing boats – hung on the porch ceiling. They reminded the boy of crystal balls he'd seen in the windows of fortune tellers. Starfish, sand dollars and a variety of shells covered the porch railing. A hand-written sign on the door read, "Abandon shoes all ye who enter here."

The cabin had two main rooms, one functioned as a bedroom, living room, and kitchen, and the other a bathroom. The only other space was in the attic, where the boy slept. To get up there, he pulled on a rope, which lowered the stairs from the ceiling.

His grandma slept late and instructed the boy not to disturb her until she awoke. So, he spent the mornings in the attic, lying on a foam mattress, reading comic books and listening to the waves lapping against the shore.

When his grandma finally rose, they'd eat breakfast and afterwards walk along the beach, always heading north. At high tide, the beach was cut off, and they couldn't go far, but when the tide was low, they would walk for a couple of hours, talking and looking for creatures.

Seagulls and sandpipers congregated in large groups. Sometimes, he saw crabs, though not as often as you'd think, considering how many discarded shells there were. His grandma told him bubbles in the sand meant there were clams below. He dug for them a few times but never found any.

There were dead and decaying things everywhere. Mounds of decomposing kelp and brown rubbery plants with tube-like tails and bulbous heads that made a satisfying pop when jumped upon. Sometimes, he'd pick one up and swing it around like a bullwhip, leaving his hands slimy and salty. The shore was littered with sand dollars. They were mostly broken, but occasionally, he would find one intact and add it to the collection on his grandma's porch.

His grandma would go back inside after their walk to make tea and read or play solitaire. The boy stayed outside. He was used to being alone but was not accustomed to being so free. He would head south to the hill. The higher ground was covered in trees and bushes, with some trails cutting through it. He walked along the trails into another realm, a place of adventure. He explored. He forged daggers and spears using his Swiss Army Knife. He became heroic. On the far side were fallen trees with yellow wood flaking off in chunks – pirate's gold, he imagined. At the top of the hill, the trees and bushes gave way to grasses and wildflowers. He could see for miles in every direction, and the boy would rest there, surveying his kingdom.

One day, he fell while climbing the hill and gashed his arm on some rocks. When he returned to the cabin, his grandma cleaned and bandaged the wound. She told him he'd be okay, getting hurt is part of growing up. Then they sat on the couch, and she showed him photos of his dad when he'd been young.

It rained a lot, even compared to Vancouver. Sometimes, it poured all day, and he would stay inside reading and looking out the window at the dark clouds over the ocean. His grandma made tea for herself and hot chocolate for him, and they played rummy.

One night, they went to a party on the beach organized by some neighbours. It was a potluck, and the boy helped his grandma make an apple crisp. One of the people there was a doctor who lived on the beach with his wife and two daughters. The boy played hide-and-seek with the girls until dinner. Then they ate salmon, crab, and scallops, followed by the apple crisp and Nanaimo bars. After dinner, there was a bonfire, and the doctor played the guitar.

One of the party guests told a story about a dead whale that had washed up on the beach a few years back. It was a novelty at first. Tourists came and took pictures. But the smell soon became so unbearable that you could hardly go onto the beach. No official person came to take care of things. The carcass just lay there for weeks, rotting and stinking. Eventually, the gases building up and trapped beneath thick layers of blubber and skin created so much pressure that the decaying corpse exploded. Chunks of rancid flesh were strewn along the beach, and the sand was stained red.

The boy's mind was buzzing as he lay in bed that night, and it took him a long time to fall asleep. He kept thinking about what the chunks of whale must have looked like, all fatty and bloody.

His dad returned at the end of the month. They stayed one last night. In the morning, the boy packed while his dad and grandma went for a walk on the beach. When they came back and were loading the boy's bags in the car, his grandma gave him one of the glass fishing balls to take home. He wondered how she knew he wanted one. Later, he would hang it up in his bedroom and lie in bed watching the light from the window reflecting off it, thinking how strange it was that fishermen from Japan had once used it to keep their nets afloat.

When they returned to Vancouver, his parents sat him down and told him they were separating. His dad had found an apartment and was moving out. He and his mom would stay in the house, at least for the present. They addressed all this gently, assuring him that they loved him and that everything would be okay, but it felt like a punch in the gut, and later he cried in his room.

He visited his grandma a few more times after that, during the part of the summers he spent with his dad. But they were just short trips. After his dad remarried and moved to Calgary, he didn't visit anymore.

The boy grew older and eventually moved to Toronto for university. After graduating, he began working, got married and had a daughter. He was busy and rarely thought of his time in Tofino. But sometimes, especially when it was raining or when he gazed at the glass fishing ball that still hung in his bedroom, he thought about Chesterman Beach.

One summer, the man took his wife and daughter to Tofino to meet his now 85-year-old grandma. He wanted to see her for what might be the last time, and he wanted his daughter to walk along the beach and experience something other than Toronto and her crowded schedule of school, piano lessons, and playdates.

He booked a room for a week at an inn that Condé Nast had recently named the best resort in Canada. The inn's website promised a combination of luxury and untamed natural beauty. He recalled that his grandma had disparaged the place as being too fancy.

They flew from Toronto to Vancouver, picked up the rental car, drove to Horseshoe Bay, and boarded the ferry. They went up to the main deck. The man took his computer out of his bag to do some work. It had been hard to get away, and he had to stay on top of things at work. His wife told him to put it away.

He returned the computer to his bag and took his daughter to the top deck. It was windy, and the man wrapped his sweater around her as they watched the waves crashing against the ferry and the mainland shrinking in the distance. "Keep your eyes on the water," the man said. "You might see a whale." The girl stared intently at the ocean but did not see one. After a bit, they went down to the cafeteria and ate hamburgers served under domed metal covers.

They got off at Nanaimo and took the winding road to Tofino. They checked in at the inn, relaxed for a few minutes, and then drove to his grandma's cabin.

At first glance, things seemed unchanged. The glass fishing balls, shells, and abandon your shoes sign were still there. The cabin, though, was smaller than he remembered. His grandma was smaller, too, and she felt brittle when he hugged her. She asked her grandson where they were staying and gave him a reproachful look when he told her.

The four of them went for a walk, heading north on the beach. All the beachfront properties except his grandma's had large boulders piled in front of them. His grandma told them this was to prevent erosion. She didn't like the boulders because they weren't part of the beach; they'd been brought from somewhere else. She had a pile of branches and sticks in front of her house that, she said, worked just fine. Every day, she went for a walk and brought back sticks to add to the pile.

She told them about the changes on the beach. About all the new houses that had been built. The man asked about the doctor with the two daughters. His grandma told him they'd moved away years ago and that the man had died last year from cancer. His grandma had gone to the funeral and seen the daughters. They lived in Vancouver and had children.

They passed a modern-looking house with large windows

facing the beach. The man admired it and asked who lived there.

His grandma grimaced. "All these rich people are here now. It's not like it was."

"Didn't Ryan Reynolds and Scarlett Johansson get married around here?" the man's wife asked.

"I don't know who they are," the grandma replied. After they walked a bit further, she said, "I don't walk as far as I used to." They started walking back. The man's daughter ran ahead, chasing birds.

When they reached the cabin, the man said he wanted to continue walking south. Leaving the others behind, he passed a group of surfers lounging on the beach. He came to the hill. He found the entrance to one of the trails. It was badly overgrown, but he pushed through. He wanted to see the place where he had adventured. To see whether the gold was still there.

He came upon a tall fence to which a "Private Property" sign was affixed. He could go no further. Peering over, he saw a large house. He imagined it must have a spectacular view of the ocean. He leaned against the fence and checked his phone. He replied to a few emails, glad his wife wasn't there to scold him.

It made sense that someone had bought the property on the hill and built a home there. It was a beautiful spot. But it bothered him that he couldn't walk through the trails, stand at the top of the hill, and look out at the ocean. It felt unfair and seemed to confirm his grandma's complaints. Things weren't the same.

He followed the fence to the road and walked back, thinking about how frail and out of touch his grandma seemed. Soon, her time would be over. Her land would be sold, and her cabin would be torn down. Someone would build a new home there with large windows overlooking the ocean, and they would bring in large boulders to replace her pile of sticks.

Back at the cabin, he found his daughter wrapped in a towel. She ran to him, laughing, "Daddy, I got wet!" The man's wife told him they'd remained on the beach after he left. The girl was exploring and collecting shells. She wandered toward the ocean. But the tide came in faster and harder than she expected, knocking her off balance. She fell, getting soaked. They took her back to the cabin, and dried her off; and then her great-grandma made her hot chocolate.

The man whistled. "Pretty exciting for your first day in Tofino."

The girl nodded. "The water was freezing!" She held out her hand and showed him a broken sand dollar and a few small shells. "Look, I found treasure!"

He took one of the shells from her. At first, he only pretended to examine it to humour her. But then he saw how it curled in on itself in a perfect spiral, and he felt the creamy smoothness of its inner side. "Pretty cool," he said, handing it back to her.

The girl took the shell and beamed. "I told Granny she can have this one for her porch."

The man noticed a small cut on the girl's wrist and pointed to it. "What happened?"

"I cut myself on a rock when I fell."

He rubbed the faded scar on his arm. "You'll be okay. That kind of thing happens around here."

The girl smiled. "Can we go exploring and collect more shells after I finish my hot chocolate?"

The man smiled and nodded.

ME

By Koker Christensen

Me woke up.

It found itself lying in a sheltered area near some rocks. It saw the brightness of the sky above and felt the hardness of the ground below. It noticed that it was hungry, so it got up and moved to an open area to look for food.

Me heard noises and knew they must be coming from nearby. But Me did not see anything of concern, so it kept looking for food. Me eventually found some in the ground. It took a lot of digging and pulling to get at, and there was only a little.

As Me was eating, a scaly thing appeared from behind a rock and approached Me. It was moving quickly, and as it came closer, Me saw that it had a sharp part sticking out. The thing lunged at Me. Me moved to one side, narrowly avoiding the sharp part. Me slashed with its own sharp part. The thing hissed and started leaking where it had been cut. Me moved quickly away, abandoning the food. The scaly thing did not follow.

Once Me was a safe distance away, it went back to looking for food. Later, Me saw a scaly thing in the distance. Me did not know whether it was the one from before or a different one. Me hurried away in the opposite direction, wishing to avoid another encounter.

Me did not find any more food.

Me noticed that it was getting dark and looked for a safe place to rest. It found a sheltered area near some rocks and tucked itself into a small nook. Soon, it was completely dark. Me was hungry but did not venture out of the nook. It stayed very still and listened to the noises. Some were noises Me had heard earlier, when it was light. Others were new. A few were very loud. Me wondered what type of things made loud noises like that and whether they had sharp parts.

Me woke up.

It found itself in a small nook between some rocks. It wriggled out and began to move about. Me was very hungry and started looking for food. There was nothing nearby. Just rocks and dirt. Me wandered, growing increasingly hungry.

Me heard a screeching noise and looked up. There was a thing in the sky. It seemed to be far off, and Me could not tell how big it was. Me hid behind a rock. When Me could no longer hear the screeching noise, it peeked out. It did not see the thing in the sky, so it left the rock and continued looking for food.

After a while, Me spotted a smaller thing resting in the shade under a tree. It was shiny and was making a soft clicking noise. Me approached slowly so as not to startle the smaller thing, but it saw Me coming and hurried away. Me sped up, trying to catch it. The smaller thing was fast, and Me could not close the gap. Me chased it for some time. Me worried that it was using a lot of energy and might not catch the smaller thing.

Eventually, the smaller thing began to tire and slow down. Me was tiring too, but not as quickly. Me caught up to the smaller thing, which then curled up in a ball.

Me poked the ball; the outside was hard. Me used its sharp part to jab the ball, but the shell was too thick to pierce. Me worried that the chase had been pointless.

Then Me noticed a rock lying nearby. It was medium-sized, and one of the ends was pointed. Me picked up the rock and brought the pointed end down on the smaller thing. Nothing happened. Me brought the rock down again, harder this time. There was a cracking noise, and the smaller thing squealed and started to leak a little. Me brought the rock down three more times as hard as it could. There was a cracking noise and a squealing noise each time, and the last time, a squishy noise. Then, the smaller thing unfurled. It was leaking a lot now. The soft bits were easy to get at, and Me ate until it was full.

Me rested after it had eaten. It looked over at what was left of the smaller thing. There was a smashed shell and the insides that Me had not finished. Some tiny things had crawled inside the shell and were eating the leftovers.

A group of other things started arriving. They were bigger than the tiny things that were already eating, but not as big as Me. One of these other things on its own was not a concern. But Me did not like that there were so many of them, so Me moved on.

A while later, it started to get dark, and Me decided to find a place to rest. There were some bushes nearby. Me crawled inside one of them and cleared a space.

Me woke up.

It moved out of the bush and looked around. There were some other bushes nearby, but no obvious food. It moved away from the bushes and started looking for something to eat.

Me saw a thing in the sky once and saw scaly things on the ground twice. Me hid each time until the thing was gone.

Me did not find anything to eat. When it started to get dark, Me found a place among some rocks. The place was not very protected, and Me was very cold once it was dark.

Me woke up.

It found itself among some rocks. It was cold and very hungry. It heard strange noises, so stayed very still. Once the noises stopped, Me moved out of the rocks and began looking for food. Eventually, it found some food growing on a bush and started eating.

While Me was eating, it heard a squeaky noise. Me turned and saw a small thing approaching. Me considered trying to catch and eat the small thing, but Me had a good bush for eating and it did not feel like a long chase. It turned back to the bush and continued eating.

The small thing moved closer to Me, and Me stopped eating to look at it again. The small thing looked at the bush where Me was eating, then looked back at Me and squeaked. Me stepped away from the bush and made a tutting sound. The small thing moved in and started eating from the bush. Me watched for a moment, then turned and moved away.

After a while, Me heard the squeaky noise again and looked

behind. The small thing was there, looking at Me. Me ignored it and continued moving about. The small thing followed Me.

When it started getting dark, Me looked for a place to rest. It found a hole beside a tree and climbed in. The small thing climbed in too and lay next to Me. Me thought about forcing the small thing out; this was Me's hole. But there was enough room for both of them, and it was warmer lying beside the small thing. Me looked up and saw dots of light in the black sky. At first, Me could only see a few of them, but after it adjusted to the dark, it saw that there were many of them. The small thing made a churring sound and moved closer to Me.

Me woke up.

It found itself in a hole near a tree, lying beside the small thing.

Me left the hole, and the small thing followed. They moved about, looking for food. All they found were a few tiny things crawling on the ground. They ate them but were still hungry. They moved about, looking for more food, but did not find anything else.

When it started to get dark, Me and the small thing looked for a place to rest. They found some tall grass and nestled in. The grass was soft. The small thing moved close to Me, and they lay together, looking up at the sky. Me could see the dots of light again. The small thing started making the churring sound. Me found itself making the same sound without even meaning to. Me dimly recalled this sound from a long time ago, when Me was small. Me remembered being with others and feeling safe, but it was hard to remember more than that. Me looked over at the small thing and thought that it was like Me when Me was small.

Me woke up.

It found itself amidst tall grass, lying beside small Me.

They left the grass to find food. They looked for a long time but did not find anything. They became very hungry. Me saw some trees in the distance and thought there might be things there to eat. There were no rocks or bushes between where they were and the trees – they would be exposed the whole way. But there was no food where they were. Me made a tutting sound and started moving towards the trees. Small Me followed.

After travelling for a while, they came upon a small thing slithering on the ground. It was also heading toward the trees. Me watched while small Me, using its sharp part, flailed at the slithery thing. Small Me was clumsy and missed three times; the slithery thing was getting away. Me moved over to help. But small Me tried again and did not miss this time. The slithery thing was cut and started violently jerking about. Small Me stepped on it to keep it in place, then brought its sharp part down on the slithery thing, slicing it in two. Small Me speared one part of the slithery thing. The other part slithered away. Me joined small Me, and they ate. Then, they continued moving toward the trees.

They were getting close when they heard the screeching noise.

Me looked up and saw a thing circling in the sky. Me looked at small Me and made a tutting noise. They sped up. The screeching noise got louder as the thing in the sky circled lower. They were moving as fast as they could now. Me looked up again and saw that the thing was right above them. Its claws were extended, and Me could see how large and sharp they were. Me was scared. Me looked over at small Me and could see that it was scared too.

The thing swooped down so that its claws were right above small Me. Me lunged sideways, knocking into the thing's claws before it could get small Me. The thing screeched and flew back up. Me looked down and saw that it was leaking.

The trees were very close now. They were almost there. Me heard the screeching noise again. It looked up and saw the thing in the sky circling again. Me kept hurrying, but it was tired and was falling behind small Me. Me saw small Me look back. Small Me was looking just past Me with a scared look on its face. Me knew that the thing from the sky must be right behind. Then, it heard the screeching noise again. It was louder than anything Me had ever heard.

Small Me turned away and kept moving towards the trees as fast as it could. It heard the screeching noise and then the shrieking. Small Me kept moving and did not look back. The shrieking stopped and was replaced by a low moaning. Then, there was no sound at all.

When small Me got to the trees, it tucked itself under some low branches. Only then did it dare look. It saw Me on the ground, motionless. The thing from the sky was tearing at Me with its beak. Small Me thought that if it had been the one the thing from the sky had gotten, the thing would be tearing at small Me, and Me would be the one watching. Part of small Me felt relieved. But mostly, it felt scared and very alone.

Small Me stayed motionless until it was completely dark and the thing had flown away. Small Me looked up through the branches, but there were no dots of light in the sky. Just darkness.

Me woke up.

It found itself nestled among some branches. A short distance away, it could see the remains of big Me. There was movement nearby, and Me knew that there would be things eating whatever was left of big Me. Me did not like thinking about this, so it turned away.

Me noticed that it was hungry and began moving about, looking for food.

AN HONEST DAY'S WORK

By D. Joel Dick

Abe sat on the upturned bushel basket. His bicycle lay on the nearby grass. The gravel crunched as the dark station wagon turned into the lane way. Through the door of the produce sorting barn, the edge of an orange tarp was visible. The air was heavy with the smell of ripe fruit and rotting vines from the neighbouring tomato farm, but the normal clanging machinery and buzz of Low German conversation were absent.

The dark station wagon stopped before the open barn door, and two young men in dark suits got out. Mr. Enns approached them.

"Guess you guys are in the right business, eh, completely recession-proof."

"I suppose, but not in this case. It's more a service – the government cheque won't even cover our costs, and the family won't be able to."

With that, the young men walked into the barn and towards the orange tarp.

The warmth of the afternoon had started to wane. Abe sat alone on the upturned basket. His mind was lost in the recall of those long minutes when he had heard the sirens as the fire truck made its way north from town on Highway 77 – those minutes when he had still hoped for a miracle, when he'd heard Elsie scream, and Jacob shouting desperately for Simon to turn off the auger.

Abe had turned in time to see Tyrone caught by the drawstring of his hoodie and pulled into the auger. Simon managed to disengage the PTO – the shaft that transferred power from the tractor to the auger – and Abe and Elsie pulled Tyrone loose and started CPR, but even then, he knew it was useless. The drawstring had cut deeply into Tyrone's throat, and a metallic smell had filled the air.

Jacob had fled the barn and could be heard throwing up behind the shed, even after the firefighters, followed by the ambulance, had arrived.

The coroner in his blue Saab had come and gone. The ambulance had pulled away empty hours ago by now. Abe sat still and stared at the tarp. He watched as the young men from Reid's Funeral Home pulled back the tarp and, with as much dignity as possible, wrestled Tyrone's corpse onto a stretcher and into the Ford station wagon.

By now, the police would have advised the consulate, and the consulate would have made a phone call to Jamaica. Like when Abe's sister fell ill with a fever and died when he was just a child or when his cousin was killed in a traffic accident in Texas. He was sure that somewhere in Jamaica, neighbours had gathered, bringing casseroles (well, maybe not casseroles), hugging the young woman who was now a widow, and telling Tyrone's young daughter that it was God's plan even if it was hard to understand.

Why did people always feel the need to give an answer even when it was obvious there wasn't one, or at least not one that made any sense?

Abe hadn't known Tyrone well, but they both lived at the motel during the season. Abe, like the other Mennonites from Mexico, was a Canadian citizen. His people had come to Manitoba in the 1870s and then left for Mexico after a fight with the government over sending their children to public schools. They had retained their Canadian citizenship and passed it down to children and grandchildren.

Therefore, they could travel easily back to Leamington to work in the tomato fields and greenhouses. Most brought their families, and many now lived in Essex County full-time. They had their own churches – not like the liberal churches of the Russian Mennonites who owned the farms, but proper churches. Abe's wife and children stayed home in Mexico. He had lived at the motel during the summer and fall for the last six years.

The motel was full of Jamaican workers on temporary visas. Their families, like Abe's, were home, far away, and he felt a kinship with them. He rarely made it to church and didn't spend too much time away from the farm with his Low German-speaking countrymen, and he rarely joined his labouring brethren at the motel as they drank their Saturday evening away in the parking lot. But he'd gotten to know Tyrone enough to wave hello.

When Tyrone fractured his foot working at an orchard, he was let go by the farmer. The Jamaican Liaison Service, a Canadian-based agency of the Jamaican government, gave Tyrone three days to find a job or fly home. His visa only allowed him to stay in Canada if he was working, and the Jamaican Liaison Service was a good partner to Canada, enforcing the rules and getting injured workers quickly out of the country.

Abe put in a good word and got Tyrone a job sorting produce. He wouldn't have to move around much, and the doctor at the emergency room had said he could stand with the walking boot on. Mr. Enns had even paid Tyrone one week in advance so he could pay for the boot.

Now, seated on the upturned basket in the immediate aftermath of the tragedy, Abe recalled the vision of blood staining the concrete floor as Tyrone's eyes bulged and clouded over. He knew that most of the machines were still running and that voices had been shouting in English and Low German as people sprinted to help or to protect themselves from the sight. It must have been loud, as the barn always is, but, in his memory, there was no noise except Elsie counting in German. Abe had pushed on the dead man's chest while she counted, then paused for her to breathe into Tyrone's mouth.

What had been only minutes from when Abe first heard the sirens of the fire engine to when the firefighters took over felt like hours, while the hours that followed, as he watched the employees from the funeral home load their cargo, felt like minutes.

The investigator from the Ministry of Labour had come in

his white Ford F-150. Abe stood close by as Mr. Enns explained that it was farm policy that the guard piece around the auger be in place at all times.

It was also true that the workers in the produce sorting barn were paid by the piece, and the guard never stayed in place long, as it slowed the work. From time to time, Mr. Enns would insist that the guard be put back in place, but he rarely noticed when it was removed. That morning, Mr. Enns had spoken to Tyrone, telling him what was expected of him. The conversation took place three and a half feet from the unguarded auger.

Why on earth had Tyrone been wearing a hoodie? It made no sense. The calendar said September, but the sun insisted it was still August. Stupid. Careless to have a drawstring around the machinery. He must have known that from working in the orchard. Surely, someone had warned him about the auger. Just last summer, it took two of Anita's fingers.

Mr. Enns would have to pay a fine, but nothing more. The investigation was easy and quick. Workers had removed the guard. "The removal was unauthorized, but management should have been more vigilant," the ministry's lawyer would advise a justice of the peace six months later. Mr. Enns wouldn't be there, but his lawyer would agree, and the fine would be set and ordered paid within 30 days.

Tyrone's red Ohio State hoodie wasn't even torn. The string had caught, and the auger wound it tight, first choking Tyrone and then tearing into his skin and finally severing the artery. Yet the fabric of the sweatshirt remained intact.

Earlier, as the firefighters and the paramedics continued pro forma CPR while awaiting confirmation from the coroner that the victim was dead, Abe heard the voices: "Ya well, you got to be more careful around the auger," followed by "Yeah for sure." But he lacked the energy to tell them to shut the fuck up.

Later, Simon addressed Abe directly, "Since we've got the afternoon off, we are going to the Family Kitchen on Erie Street. Do you want to join me and the girls? It will be a nice afternoon. You should come."

"No. It's not a damn vacation day. The body is still lying right there," is what Abe remembered saying, his indignation both justified and clear. A mumbled "No, thanks" is all Simon remembered hearing.

Abe couldn't help but think of the house or apartment in Jamaica filled with grief. He didn't even know what part of the country Tyrone was from. He didn't know Tyrone's wife's name. Tyrone had shown him the picture of his two girls, nine and four. He couldn't remember their names, but much later that night, as he helped to pack up Tyrone's belongings at the motel, he would sit and hold that photo and think of his own little Maria and Ruth. It would be then, with his girl's blonde hair in mind, that he would cry.

The station wagon pulled away. Mr. Enns closed the barn door.

"Everyone else has gone, Abe. You'd best go, too. The days are getting shorter, and the sunlight won't last. You know, it isn't safe biking in the dark, and I can't be down two men Monday morning."

Mr. Enns' voice trailed off. He swallowed hard. "I know you knew him. I didn't mean anything. Just be safe, Abe." With that, Mr. Enns turned and walked back towards the house.

"I know, Sir."

Had Abe actually uttered the words or only thought them?

He couldn't be sure.

He mounted the old CCM Supercycle and pedalled up the lane. He could see Mr. Enns pushing his young son on the swing and Mrs. Enns hanging laundry on the line.

He peddled slowly south on 77. The air was heavy but cooler now that the sun was setting. The roadside stands offered cucumbers and tomatoes for sale. He passed the usual lineup of cars that snaked around the Tim Hortons drive-thru.

In fifteen minutes, he'd be back at the motel. Word will have already spread, but the men at the hotel will want him to repeat the story. And he'll be happy to relive the day's events surrounded by Tyrone's friends. He'll feel a kinship with men who, for years, have lived beside him, separated only by the thin walls of Rymal's Motel. For an hour or so, they will all be bonded by Tyrone's death, and Abe will belong.

An hour and a half from now, he'll be helping to pack up Tyrone's belongings. Abe will hold that photograph of two small girls on a beach. In the photo, one has her curly hair held back by an orange headband, and the other is wearing tight braids and a white dress. Then, he will quietly excuse himself. He will stand behind the motel and think of his Maria. He will recall Ruth as a baby falling asleep on his shoulder. He will cry.

He won't sob or make a scene. He will quietly indulge a few tears as he thinks of his little girls and those two other girls posing for a photo on the beach.

Now, he is simply pedalling his bike. Surprised, somehow, to see that life is going on normally throughout town.

Later, the men in the motel parking lot will invite Abe to join them to toast Tyrone's memory. He will politely decline, reminding them that he doesn't drink. He wouldn't be able to think of anything to say in any event. He'd lived in a room next to Tyrone for three and a half months. He'd waved hello. He'd remarked upon the weather, and Tyrone had told him that even July wasn't hot enough for him. "Sure, is humid enough, yet," Abe had replied. Then, Tyrone had gotten hurt and needed a job, and Abe helped him get work at the Enns farm. Not enough material for a meaningful toast, even if Abe had wanted to join in. Other than the details of Tyrone's death, Abe won't have anything else to say.

But that won't be until later, after sunset, after Tyrone's room has been packed up for the men from the consulate, who are coming from Windsor in the morning. For now, Abe simply pedalled his bike towards the motel and let his mind focus only on the road in front of him.

Hours from now, Abe will realize it was too late to call his wife, and he will send a series of text messages instead. He will also text his uncle and invite himself to church. He hadn't been inside a church for over a year, but looking down at his phone, he will realize that he had made a plan for the morning and asked for a ride.

He will fall asleep to the sounds of music from the motel parking lot as the once sombre gathering gets louder with each drink consumed in Tyrone's honour. The quiet embraces and condolences of the evening will morph into rowdy and bawdy stories by midnight. The music will be turned up. The collection taken up for the widow will be forgotten, at least for the night, and laughter will roll in waves as the men recall Tyrone's adventures. Abe doesn't have any stories to tell, and he will listen to all of this from his bed behind a closed door.

Tomorrow is Sunday, and he will join his uncle, his aunt

and his cousins at church. He will even stay for the potluck lunch and join the game of softball.

He will wake in the early morning hours with the old Sunday school hymn, "Gott ist die Liebe," playing as the sound-track to his dream of Tyrone's lifeless body. Except it was his face, not Tyrone's, that he sees in the dream. And the photo-graph at the beach is of Maria and Ruth. He will shake himself and get out of bed to piss.

Tomorrow afternoon, after he returns home from church, the potluck and the softball game, he will call home, and the conversation with his girls will seem more sacred and special than usual.

Monday, he will ride his bike north on Highway 77 and go to work.

PHOTO FINISH

By D. Joel Dick

"Good morning, Representative-elect Foote," teased Ted as he walked into the room.

"Hard to believe that it's been a week already. Congratulations to you, Mr. Stillwater. You ran a picture-perfect campaign for us. We shouldn't have won." Kerry paused to put her coffee on the table and leaned back as Ted sat in the chair across from her.

They both still carried the glow of winning a race that no one thought they could. The district had a high floor but a low ceiling of Democratic votes. Its smallish urban center was blue enough, but then it stretched out into inflexibly red territory. The north of the district was populated with evangelical voters, who historically turned out heavily and voted overwhelmingly for the Republican candidate, no matter who that candidate had been. The western portion was sparsely populated farmland.

The result was a district that one political pundit called "Fool's gold for Team Blue" until Kerry Foote put together a coalition of voters that delivered the 11th to the Democrats by 742 votes or just over half of a percent.

"Ted, you did the impossible. You really ran an amazing campaign: good paid TV, great earned media, top-notch voter contact. Thank you."

Stillwater laughed, "You've got to be lucky to be good, right?"

"Yes, and we were that, weren't we?" Kerry responded. "I mean, the whole thing with Lloyd's past drug use coming out the Wednesday before the election and then that photo of him with the shirtless twink kissing his cheek and, in the fore-ground, a table that appears to have cocaine on it. I may have hated his policies, but I always liked him. That photo must have devastated his wife and kids.

"That picture won the election. The raw votes downtown in the white liberal precincts and the Spanish-speaking neigh-bourhoods are very close to what our side got two years ago. Hardly up at all.

"And the western part of the district barely budged either. But the evangelical turnout cratered."

"Probably true, but that is politics, never dull," Ted replied.

"Still, it doesn't quite add up, does it? I mean, our Lloyd is nothing if not meticulous, and I just don't buy that he is some kind of secret closet case," Kerry said.

"Well, I gu–"

"Ted, let me tell you a story," Kerry interjected. "It isn't like Lloyd's history with Adderall was public knowledge, but it wasn't a closely guarded secret either. It's not entirely surprising that an alternative weekly got its hands on a twelve-year-old letter from an HR file showing Lloyd went to a rehab program. What's odd is that a reporter who was good enough to unearth that letter missed that Lloyd was in rehab for abusing prescription medication and wrote a story implying Lloyd had a problem with street drugs back in the day and maybe, just maybe, still did today. You and I both know he was using Adderall as a young lawyer to work longer hours and focus in court while he took endless notes. I don't think the guy has ever smoked a joint, let alone done coke."

Kerry paused for an instant, then added: "You were a partner at the same law firm where Lloyd worked as an associate, weren't you, Ted?"

"I'm not sure what exactly you are implying, Congresswoman," Ted seethed.

"You would have known he needed time off for treatment twelve years ago. But then, like I said, it wasn't a closely held secret," Kerry explained. "Then the ridiculous press conference with Lloyd – his mistake for sure. He was flustered and angry and made that really stupid comment about pictures.

"Then that photograph comes out on Friday."

"Just doesn't add up for me. Then I realized that the photo was from the upstairs room at Monkey Business. I mean, no prize for recognizing one of two gay bars in town, but Lloyd making that kind of mistake, being that reckless, seemed odd.

"I also remembered that the owner of Monkey Business is a huge Lloyd fan. I had asked him for a donation, and I got a speech about property taxes, sales taxes, and the old city entertainment venue tax that Lloyd helped to kill when he was on the city council. That guy is a 'log cabin' type. He could ignore the more offensive things Lloyd said because he trusted that that was part of the act. He wasn't going to take away his right to make a profit. It makes sense that Lloyd would have stopped by to thank him for his support after the debate at the Rotary Club next door during the primary.

"I got to thinking; it wouldn't take much for you, a guy active in the gay community with the human rights campaign and the fight for equal marriage, to have a friend who tends bar at Monkey Business. It is a small community. Hell, when you walked me around the village, it felt like you knew every second person.

"A smart Democratic operative might have foreseen that his former associate and current city councillor had the skills to win a crowded Republican primary. That kind of smart guy might want some security in his back pocket. That kind of smart, professional campaign manager might even think a guy who has always been a business-first Republican suddenly becoming a culture warrior to win a primary deserved a little comeuppance."

"It wouldn't be hard to predict that Lloyd might stop by the bar to thank an early supporter and small business owner. It wouldn't be hard to have a couple of friends 'mistakenly' stumble upstairs into a private party at four in the afternoon. Then, maybe a bartender working upstairs moves a table close to the bar and dumps some sugar onto a mirror. Odd, right? But things are happening quickly.

"A constituent, the guy on the right in that photo, asks an aspiring congressman having a post-debate celebratory pint for a photo. Lloyd obliges and steps forward. The constituent wraps an arm around his shoulders and nudges him so the table is in the frame. Then, just as a friend holds up his phone to get the picture, a shirtless man dashes in and kisses the politician on his cheek. Everyone laughs. The afternoon carries on, and everyone forgets about the photo."

"I think you should stop talk—"

"Then, you sit on that picture until you leak the dates of Lloyd's treatment to some poor kid five minutes out of journalism school, working for poverty wages at a weekly paper, and too green to know he is being used. And Lloyd, poor dumb Lloyd, bless his heart, goes out and says the most stupid thing possible: 'If I was using drugs, there would be pictures.' That, you couldn't have planned; he certainly gift-wrapped that.

"Then, someone sends Channel Five that photo, just in time for it to run on the Friday morning show, too late for Lloyd to fight back, and really, how can he? He looks like a closet case. I mean, he did that horrible Sunday news conference where his poor, humiliated wife had to stand beside him, and it just made him look worse. Evangelical voters stay home, and we win.

"Am I close? I mean, we won, right? Who cares if we betray our principles? Who cares if we destroy a marriage and a family? And who cares if we rely on homophobia to win? Dammit, Ted, we are supposed to be better than this. I am better than this. You had no right to do this." Kerry was yelling now.

"I had no right?" Ted barely whispered, simmering with contempt. "We didn't play by the Queensbury rules, and your delicate constitution is offended, Ms. Prim and Proper."

"Ted—"

"Shut up! I listened to your story; now you listen to me. If, and I say if, your story is true, what right do you have to tell Luis that we need to play nice? That young man worked seven days a week for you. He has lived almost his whole life in a country that doesn't want him as a citizen. All that keeps him from being sent back to a country he last saw when he was eighteen months old is an executive order that could evaporate with the next president if we don't get actual legislation. How dare you tell the Dreamers that your delicate sense of fairness trumps their right to live in the country that has been their home. How dare you tell me that abstract principles of fairness are more important than my right to marry the man I love! Really! Just stuff it, Kerry. You will vote to protect what's left of the Voting Rights Act, while Lloyd would have gutted it completely. Your feelings are not worth more than the right of Black Americans to vote. You know Lloyd advocates further deregulation in the financial sector. Fair play doesn't outrank my grandmother's right to live in her home and not be cheated out of her savings.

"So, no, I don't care how we won. I care that we won. I don't care how many interviews you give mewling in support of civility because I know how you'll vote. It isn't your right to marry, your right to live in the country you love, or your right not to get shot during a routine traffic stop that is on the line, so just get off your high horse. Or don't, I don't care. You wanted to play in the big leagues, and this isn't bean bag."

Ted stood and walked towards the door before adding, "Congratulations, Representative Foote. The folder on the table includes the resumes of the chief of staff candidates. I recommend choosing one of the top three. They all have experience at the state level and will be able to handle Washington. You are going to need help in the big leagues, Ma'am."

THROUGH THE SHADOWS

By D. Joel Dick

The muted orange and violet of sunrise glowed on the horizon as he entered the bus station, walking purposefully to locker 17B. He opened the locker and withdrew a worn blazer, a starched white shirt, grey slacks, and brown patent leather shoes. Closing the locker, he left the station carrying the blazer and pants in his right hand, the shirt in his left, and the leather shoes stuffed into his battered red and black backpack.

He made his way north toward the YMCA, and his lips moved nearly imperceptibly as he whispered, "Though the fig tree may not blossom, nor fruit be on the vines." Arriving at the YMCA, he was relieved to see Rashid behind the desk. Rashid was always kind enough to look the other way, enabling him to slide past the turnstile and down the hall to the locker room and the rare treat of a warm, unhurried shower. Luxuriating under the warm water, he steeled himself against the coming day: he had no desire to be around people or to step inside a church, and yet today, he planned to do both.

Stepping from the shower and towelling off, he saw him, with his dark hair and glasses, staring wordlessly and menacingly from across the room. Seated by the lockers, the young man simply stared back, a silent warning – quiet and watching. "Well, let him follow me," he thought. "I've got other concerns today."

He pulled the cheap, disposable razor across his face, brushed his hair with his fingers, and pulled on the blazer. He stuffed his tattered jeans and blue tee into the backpack and headed for the exit. The sun was now fully up, and the air heavy with humidity and the promise of heat.

Thrusting his hand into the unfamiliar pocket of the woollen slacks, he felt for the Loonie, two quarters, and a dime that he hoped were still there. Finding them, he entered the coffee shop triumphantly.

Small coffee in hand, and with his backpack slung over one shoulder, he trudged north.

His thoughts turned to his dear younger sister, "Naked came I out of the womb. Naked shall I return." He walked on, feeling the first hint of a blister on his right foot.

Finally, he reached a small parkette and settled onto a bench facing the street. There he was, the same young man from this morning, his blonde hair cut close. He was pretending to read a newspaper, which obscured his face, but it was him. Following. Watching.

Clearly, they were just watching today. If they had planned worse, it would have happened by now, and he knew he could evade the watchers after the service.

Across the street, people began to file into the church. It must have been 10:40 by now, but he would wait. The church parking lot was full, and cars were parked down the side street. Relatively speaking, she had been young, and the end was so sudden that it was not surprising that the turnout was large. He watched and waited. He watched more people enter the church. Men in suits, despite the July heat. Young children in their mothers' arms, laughing, oblivious to the solemnity of the day.

Shortly after eleven o'clock, he stood and crossed the street. He pulled open the door and entered the church, standing at the edge of the lobby just outside the stifling sanctuary. The last notes of the choir faded, and the preacher stepped to the pulpit.

> The Lord is my shepherd; I shall not want.
> He maketh me to lie down in green pastures: he
> leadeth me beside the still waters.
> He restoreth my soul: he leadeth me in the
> paths of righteousness for his name's sake.
> Yea, though I walk through the valley of the
> shadow of death, I will fear no evil: for thou art
> with me; thy rod and thy staff they comfort me.
> Thou preparest a table before me in the
> presence of mine enemies: thou anointest my
> head with oil; my cup runneth over.
> Surely goodness and mercy shall follow me
> all the days of my life: and I will dwell in the
> house of the Lord forever.

The sermon continued. The choir sang. They rose and sat. His sister's daughter tearfully stood behind the pulpit and eulogized. The congregation sang in harmony. He stood rooted to his spot just beyond the threshold of the sanctuary. He had not stood still indoors for this length of time in decades. He stood and tried to listen, but his eyes were drawn back again and again to the polished oak.

> There the wicked cease from troubling and
> there the weary rest.
> There the prisoners rest together; they hear not
> the voice of the oppressor.
> The small and great are there; and the servant
> is free from his master.

Without realizing it, he had joined the hymn together with the congregation, the words finding their way to his lips from some deep recess of his mind where they had lain hidden together with the remnants of his childhood. The pastor stood and recited the ancient prayer. Concluding, "…is the power and the glory forever and ever, Amen."

The congregation stood. The young men came forward, flanking the coffin, the woman from the funeral home leading them as they wheeled the casket up the aisle. Still, he stood. The congregation, turning to follow the progress of the body, could see him now. Still, he stood and fought the urge to flee the danger of being confined by walls.

As the pallbearers passed him, he reached out and touched the polished timber and grasped a single rose from the spray, pulling it loose as his sister moved past him. The eldest son of his youngest sister stepped towards him and gripped him tightly in a bear hug.

His mind screamed, "My breath kindles coals, and a flame comes forth with my breath." But, of course, he said nothing. Every fibre of his being wished to be loose, to run, to flee the danger. His mind was racing; panic spiked his heart rate; claustrophobia pressed down. His body and his soul urged him to accept and return the hug. He wanted to cry and melt into his nephew's arms. He simply stood statue-still, neither returning the hug nor fleeing.

The eldest son of his youngest sister spoke: "Thank you for coming. She would have wanted you here. It was so sudden." With that, his nephew was swept along with the crowd exiting the sanctuary and following the procession to the hearse.

He had done his duty. He turned and found an emergency exit away from the parking lot and hurried into the alley. "I am alone now," he thought. "I will redeem them all. My suffering will be the balm."

He could not see them, but he felt their proximity. He had to move quickly. He hoped that the loading of the casket into the hearse on the far side of the church would provide enough of a distraction for him to evade them yet again.

He strode quickly to the east. Passing between the yellowed brick of the school and its neighbouring bungalow and squeezing through the gap in the rusted chain link fence, he descended the dirt path into the ravine. It was July, and school was out, so there were no groups of furtive smokers or teens clumsily coupling in the trees. He walked further into the ravine, drinking in the solitude. The city was still close at hand, but he was safer here among the foxes, raccoons, coyotes, and mosquitoes. He understood the eternal cycle of the trees and animals nurturing each other with their lives and deaths. The whir of a drone reached his ear, and he ducked under the trees, unseen.

The sun was past its apex, and the breeze was brisk with the energy of the approaching storm. The buzz of the cicada was noticeable in its sudden absence.

A single red-tailed hawk soared in lazy circles, floating effortlessly above the trees. The raptor hung in the sky, its wings still and fixed in place. He knew that his sympathy should lie with the trembling rodents that shared the earth beneath the trees with him. Still, he was drawn to the grace of the bird's flight, its coiled violence implied but not yet spoken, as it floated unperturbed by either the approaching storm or the terror of the squirrels.

He didn't have the luxury of ignoring the coming deluge, and so he looked back to the path, the hawk still looping in circles. If the killing dive ever came, he was no longer there to see it. He finally reached the official city trail that snaked along the bottom of the ravine. Pausing next to a small wood and metal footbridge that crossed the creek, he listened. He heard nothing and was satisfied that for at least one more day, he had evaded the watchers.

Crossing to the midpoint, he released the single rose into the water. "You are free of tribulations now," he whispered. Then he strode to the other side of the bridge. He pulled his soiled jeans and tee shirt from his pack. Stripping quickly, he stuffed his white shirt, tattered jacket, pants, and leather shoes into the pack in an attempt to keep them clean – or at least from getting any dirtier. He pulled on his jeans and New Balance sneakers. He jumped down the embankment and scampered under the bridge. Crawling through the dirt and sheltered by the bridge, he heard the first drops of rain strike the boards above his head just as a peel of thunder echoed in the valley.

He drew his tattered notebook and pencil from the front pocket of his backpack and began to write:

There is a path which no fowl knows and which
the vulture has not seen, the fierce lion has
not trod upon it. He binds the floods with the
banks of the river and sets the stars into the
night sky the things that are hidden He brings
forth to light.

The storm had now passed, and the daylight was fading. For the moment, he was safe. He tucked his backpack under his head as a pillow. He got the few hours sleep he longed for, awoke to return his dress clothes to their home in the bus station locker, and spent the rest of the night walking – always moving through the shadows to keep ahead of the watchers.

68

A COMPLICATED CASE

By Edan Howell

The conference was over for the day, and she was deeply exhausted. The speakers had been boring, and her colleague had been annoying, making comments throughout the day that singed her nerves. She'd called home on the way back to her room, feeling drained. All was well, but the kids had way too much energy for her to talk long. She was thankful for a night away from home. Her feet were hurting, work emails were piling up, and it was hot in the hallway outside her door. Where on earth was the hotel room key in the wilds of her purse?

She opened the door. The room was cool and smelled pleasant. He was reading in the chair. She honestly would have preferred a moment to herself, but it was nice that he was waiting for her. He lit up, obviously happy to see her. She smiled inwardly and threw her coat and purse on the bed. He was a good man for her. Hard, but gentle. Mature, but playful. Something in him was a little damaged, but he was competent and sure of himself. Best of all, the love he had for her was direct, simple, honest, and intense. The situation was hopelessly complicated, but his feelings for her were not. They were strong. Steady. Something solid that she could depend on.

He asked about her day, but she wasn't in the mood to go over it, muttering something trite in response. He was still gazing at her. Right at her. The attention was nice. She turned to the mirror and asked about plans for the evening as she unbuttoned her blouse, casually pulling it off. She turned to look at him, but he didn't answer, still looking intensely at her in her black bra and skirt. Something was stirring in her, and the blood was radiating to her skin. She pretended not to notice his eyes on her. She undid the clasp and pulled down the zipper of her skirt slowly, wiggling a little to help it fall seductively from her hips. She stepped out and turned away again. Normally, she would have kicked her heels off by now, but she knew they made her legs look good. That morning, she had seen herself in the mirror and found a few things she wasn't happy with. She preferred to see herself in his eyes.

She should have been cold with so little on, but her skin was tingling and warm. His gaze was still locked on her, and she felt her power. She put up a finger and almost imperceptibly motioned for him to come to her. He got up and closed the space more quickly than she expected. "Take your shirt off," she said. It was gone in a moment.

She always enjoyed his body, hers whenever she wanted. She put her hand on his chest to feel the strangeness of the muscles and ran it up over his shoulder. His chest heaved, and he pulled her close. She was physically small and had no chance to resist. She looked up at him with a smile. She continued to trace her hand over his shoulders very gently and used her other hand to undo his belt. He was looking at her fiercely now, and she had a sense that this wasn't going to be under control for much longer. She softened her grip on him so that she was barely touching him. He was breathing deeply, but her gentleness had worked, and he seemed a little bit calmer. She stroked him as softly as she could, barely touching him at all. She kissed him once very gently, then licked his lips forcefully, messily.

His fingers were gentle as he unclasped her bra, and suddenly, her breasts were exposed to the cool air. He couldn't take his eyes off her. She put one hand on his chin to pull his eyes off her breasts and kissed him hungrily. He put his fingers in her hair and enveloped her head in his hands. She took a step forward to sit on the bed. He kicked off his pants without taking his eyes off her. She lay down, stroked herself sensually, and enjoyed the sensation of being naughty in front of him.

"Take off my panties," she whispered, loving the sultry sound of her voice. She raised her legs, brought them together, and rested her ankles on his shoulder. He tucked his thumbs under the black lace and tugged the panties off.

She casually slipped off her shoes, pushed his head back, and slid into the middle of the bed. She touched her lips to signal that he should kiss her. She closed her eyes and lost herself in his lips.

There was no shyness left in her now. She licked her lips slowly, provocatively.

They settled into a perfect rhythm that engulfed both of them. She felt hot, and he was enraptured. She felt a wave gathering in her, building and building until it heaved and crashed out. She felt warm light pouring over her skin, small tears squeezed out of her eyes, and gasping spurts of laughter burst forth.

Suddenly, the world lost its balance,and there was no such thing as up. She felt her body hoisted as though weightless in an avalanche. It was fantastic! She let her body be bounced around while she enjoyed the sensation of having him take her. She had no control and could hear the air in her lungs being forced out of her with each thrust. She felt the muscles in his arms squeezing her and pumping her body. Enjoying her. She found one of his arms and put her hand on it to steady herself. She heard him grunting, then suddenly exploded. He was gasping and sweating. His grip began to loosen, though his breathing was still heavy. She felt his sweat on her skin, and the world came back into focus. She slumped into the embracing, comforting warmth of his body.

He lay her down softly on her back and gently brushed stray strands of hair from her face. His chest and shoulders still heaved massively with every breath, but he was clearly spent. Her heart felt huge. She held out her arms to him. He wrapped her up and nuzzled his face into her neck. "I love you," he gasped. "I love you so much." She smiled inwardly and ran her fingernails gently through his hair.

APPENDIX

The following is a list of short stories, essays, and biblical passages read and discussed by the authors:

Margaret Atwood	Happy Endings
Isaac Babel	My First Goose
David Bezmozgis	A New Gravestone for an Old Grave
Bible	David and Goliath (1 Samuel 17: 1-58)
Bible	ExodusFromEgypt (Exodus 1-19)
Ambrose Bierce	An Occurrence at Owl Creek Bridge
Jason Brown	A Faithful but Melancholy Account of Several Barbarities
Italo Calvino	Difficult Loves
Italo Calvino	The Adventures of the Married Couple
Raymond Carver	Cathedral
Ted Chaing	Exhalation

Ted Chaing	The Merchant and the Alchemist's Gate
Ted Chaing	What's Expected of Us
Anton Chekhov	The Lady With the Little Dog
Ta-Nehisi Coates	So That's Just One of My Losses
Harlan Ellison	I Have No Mouth, and I Must Scream
William Faulkner	Barn Burning
Richard Feynman	The Relation of Science and Religion
Gabriel Garcia Marquez	Eyes of a Blue Dog
Nikolai Gogol	The Overcoat
Nadine Gordimer	The Moment Before the Gun Went Off
Nathaniel Hawthorne	Young Goodman Brown
Earnest Hemmingway	Big Two-Hearted River
Earnest Hemmingway	The Killers
Earnest Hemmingway	The Short Happy Life of Francis Macomber
Earnest Hemmingway	The Snows of Kilimanjaro
Earnest Hemmingway	Three Day Blow
Shirley Jackson	The Lottery
W. W. Jacobs	The Monkey's Paw
James Joyce	After the Race
James Joyce	The Real Thing
Franz Kafka	A Hunger Artist
Walter Kim	The Spaceship and the Moose
Thomas King	77 Fragments of a Familiar Ruin
Maxine Hong Kingston	No Name Woman
Rudyard Kipling	Benefit of Clergy

DH Lawrence	A Rocking-Horse Winner
Sidura Ludvig	You Are Not What We Expected
Bernard Malamud	Jewbird
Katherine Mansfield	The Garden Party
Anthony Marra	The Leopard
Guy de Maupassant	The Necklace
Alistair McLeod	The Closing Down of Summer
Claire Messud	Disappearing Ink
Alice Munro	Hateship, Friendship, Courtship, Loveship, Marriage
Alice Munro	Royal Beatings
Alice Munro	Save the Reaper
Alice Munro	The Bear Came Over the Mountain
Alice Munro	The Beggar Maid
Alice Munro	The Vandals
H.H. Munro	The Open Window
Vladimir Nabokov	Symbols and Signs
Flannery O'Connor	A Good Man is Hard to Find
Flannery O'Connor	Good Country People
George Orwell	Benefit of Clergy: Some Notes on Salvador Dali
George Orwell	Why I Write
Grace Paley	An Interest in Life
Krzysztof Pelc	Green Velvet
Edgar Allan Poe	The Cask of Amontillado
Edgar Allan Poe	The Fall of the House of Usher
Kristen Roupenian	Cat Person
Lionel Shriver	Lefty Lingo
Aleksander Solzhenitsyn	Apricot Jam

John Steinbeck	The Chrysanthemums
Souvankham Thammavongsa	Slingshot
Leo Tolstoy	The Wood Felling: A Cadet's Story
Anuja Vaarghese	Meditations on a Lake
Tobias Wolff	Bullet in the Brain
David Foster Wallace	Brief Interviews With Hideous Men #6
David Foster Wallace	Shipping Out
David Wallace-Wells	The Uninhabitable Earth
Alejandro Zambra	Screen Time

THE AUTHORS

After graduating from Queen's University **Evan Bruce** went into accounting in Toronto. He and his wife Sarah have two amazing kids. He loves camping, carpentry, and cooking.

Koker Christensen grew up in Vancouver and lives in Toronto. He works as a lawyer.

D. Joel Dick is a lawyer living in Toronto with his family. He was born and raised in Essex County in South Western Ontario.

Edan Howell, a graduate of the University of Toronto Faculty of Law, is a lawyer, portfolio manager, and business leader.